William Shakespeare's

The Tempest

ADAPTED BY MARIANNA MAYER • ILLUSTRATED BY LYNN BYWATERS

chronicle books · san francisco

Type and jacket design by Tracy Sunrize Johnson.
Typeset in Bembo.
The illustrations in this book were rendered in gouache.
Manufactured in Hong Kong.

Library of Congress Cataloging-in-Publication Data
Mayer, Marianna.
    William Shakespeare's The tempest / adapted by Marianna Mayer ; illustrated by Lynn Bywaters.
        p. cm.
    ISBN 0-8118-5054-4
    1. Survival after airplane accidents, shipwrecks, etc—Juvenile fiction.
    2. Fathers and daughters—Juvenile fiction. 3. Castaways—Juvenile fiction.
        4. Magicians—Juvenile fiction. 5. Islands—Juvenile fiction. 6. Spirits—Juvenile fiction.
    I. Bywaters, Lynn. II. Shakespeare, William, 1564–1616. Tempest. III. Title.
    PR2878.T4M39 2005
    813'.54—dc22

                                        2005005352

Distributed in Canada by Raincoast Books
9050 Shaughnessy Street, Vancouver, British Columbia V6P 6E5

10 9 8 7 6 5 4 3 2 1

Chronicle Books LLC
85 Second Street, San Francisco, California 94105

www.chroniclekids.com

For Chelsea Le Moine, who would find many friends
upon this enchanted island —M. M.

To my friends and teachers at Eagle's Quest
and Silent Dragon —L. B.

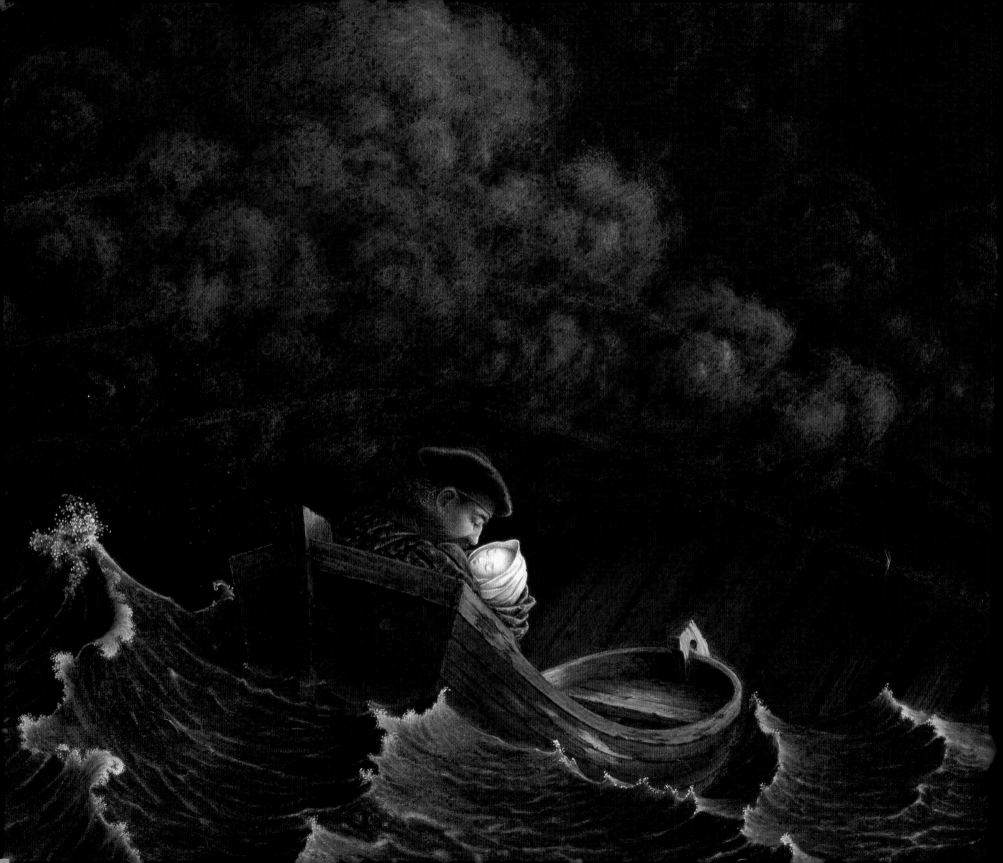

Long, long ago, there was a magician named Prospero who lived on an enchanted island with his daughter, Miranda.

Once, Prospero had been the duke of Milan, but on a rain-swept night he and his baby daughter were abducted. Thrown into an open boat, they were cast into the roaring sea and left to perish. But a loyal friend of Prospero had hidden a bundle of provisions and precious books on the magic arts inside the hull of the boat. With the help of these books, Prospero was able to guide the boat to an island paradise where he made a home for himself and his child.

All these events had occurred some twelve years ago; Miranda was a young maiden now. She remembered nothing of that terrible night, but her father never forgot. One day, Prospero vowed, he would avenge the wrongs done to him and his daughter.

Now it seemed that day had come, for the two men responsible for the crime—Prospero's brother Antonio and Alonso, the king of Naples—were onboard a sailing vessel that was passing near the island's shores.

That morning the skies had been bright blue and a steady wind had swelled the snow-white sails, carrying the ship gently over calm, sea-green waters. But as the island came in sight, a huge dark cloud loomed and the sea turned black. The startled passengers shouted in terror as a howling wind engulfed the ship in a roaring tempest.

The captain and crew struggled to control the vessel, but lashing waves propelled the ship ever closer to the island's jagged cliffs. Tossed like a toy in the angry waters, the ship crashed against the cliffs and split apart. The king, his son, and Antonio, as well as the rest of the passengers, were flung into the violent sea, at last surrendering themselves to a watery grave.

Miranda watched the terrifying spectacle from the island's shores. With tears in her eyes, she ran to seek her father in the cave that was their home. "Father," she cried, taking both his hands in hers, "if your magic art can turn the sea from its deadly course, I beg you, save these poor suffering souls upon that ship!"

"Hush, my tenderhearted child, and wipe your tears. It is I who caused this tempest," admitted her father. "It is all for you, my dearest one."

Miranda looked at him in astonishment. "For me?"

Removing his magic robe, Prospero sat down with a sigh. "It's time you know," he said. "First, I give you my promise that not one soul onboard that ship has been harmed.

"Now then," he began, "listen and I shall explain. Two men on that ship, my brother and the king of Naples, are my archenemies. Long ago, my brother, with the aid of the king, seized my dukedom and then cast me and you, an innocent baby, out upon the sea to perish."

As Miranda listened, tears welled up in her eyes. And when her father came to the end of his tale, she said, "My heart breaks for your misfortune, my dearest father. How you must have suffered. Yet why bring about the storm?"

"The wild tempest has cast my foes and their companions upon these shores," Prospero said. And seizing his magic staff, he declared with fire in his eyes, "Now I shall finally extract revenge upon these villains."

Prospero left his daughter and went at once to speak with his servant the lively wind spirit Ariel, who was invisible to all but the magician. Yet the enchanted island was not only home to Prospero and the lovely Miranda; besides Ariel and other sprites, there was Caliban, who also served the magician. He was the half-human, half-animal son of the witch Sycorax, who had ruled the island until her death.

While Sycorax lived, Ariel had been imprisoned in a tree for refusing to carry out her evil commands. After the witch's death, Ariel remained trapped within the tree until Prospero arrived. Hearing Ariel's pitiful cries, the magician used his powers to release the sprite, and from that day forward, Ariel and the other sprites accepted him as their master.

"Well, spirit," said Prospero, addressing Ariel. "I am ready for a full account of the ship and its passengers."

Delighted, the playful Ariel gave a vivid description of the storm and of the terror of the ship's company.

"Excellent!" Prospero exclaimed. "But where are they now?"

"Ferdinand, the king's son, sits weeping for the loss of his father and friends," replied Ariel with a mischievous laugh. "For he believes himself to be the sole survivor.

"At the same time," continued the sprite, "King Alonso and your faithless brother Antonio wander together on the other side of the isle. But the king's jester, Trinculo, and the king's butler, Stephano, are lost even to each other. As for the ship's captain and his crew, they sleep peacefully under a heavy spell. And the ship, though safe and sound upon the beach, has been made invisible."

"Well done!" said the magician. "In two days' time you shall serve me no longer. But now bring the prince to me so that my Miranda can meet him."

"Will I really be free?" Ariel asked. "Will you keep your promise, master?"

"Yes, yes," replied the magician. "Now go and do as I say."

While Prospero awaited the prince, he called his servant Caliban to fetch firewood. Slowly the creature crawled from his rock dwelling, cursing.

"There is wood enough," snarled the scruffy Caliban.

"What?" said Prospero. "Ungrateful brute, don't argue! Who was it who taught you speech?"

"Ha! Was you taught me," Caliban answered. "Once you petted me and treated me kind, but no more."

"That I did, until you savagely attacked my daughter," said Prospero.

"And so I would again," said Caliban, laughing wickedly.

"For that, tonight you shall be pinched by a dozen invisible hands!" threatened Prospero.

"No!" Caliban whined. "I am going to get the wood." He shuffled off, all the while muttering under his breath, "His magic is too powerful. I must obey."

Not far off, Ariel arrived unseen at the side of Prince Ferdinand. Leaning close to the youth's ear, the spirit whispered, "Quick! On your feet, my young gentleman—the beautiful lady Miranda must have a look at you. Come now and follow me!"

Then Ariel began to sing a strange and enchanting melody. Beguiled by the haunting music, Ferdinand rose at once to follow its call.

Miranda and her father were sitting under the shade of a large willow tree when she first caught sight of the young prince coming toward them. Startled, she exclaimed, "Look there, father. Is that not a spirit?"

"No, child," said Prospero, laughing. "It eats and sleeps and might even be called handsome. This young man was on the ship."

Miranda gazed in fascination. The prince was not old and gray haired like her dear father, but rather near her age and as fair as a god, in her opinion. As for Ferdinand, he believed Miranda to be some wondrous goddess of rare beauty.

Coming forward, the youth bowed respectfully. "May I humbly address this enchanted island's reigning goddess?"

"Sir," replied Miranda with a shy smile, "I am no goddess, but a mortal girl."

Before she could say more, her father stepped between them and addressed the prince sternly. "Don't think I am a fool, sir," Prospero said, feigning anger. "I know you are a spy come to do me harm."

"No, sir! You are mistaken," said the prince, shocked.

Truly, Prospero hoped that the two young people would fall
in love. But he fully intended to put a few obstacles in the path
of their courtship as a means of testing the strength of their
feelings.

"Don't deny it," demanded Prospero. "You are my prisoner,
sir. You shall be given hard labor, drink nothing but seawater,
and dead roots will be your food. Now follow me!"

"Certainly not!" exclaimed the prince. Thinking the older
man no match for him, he prepared to stand his ground. But
when Prospero waved his staff, the youth was unable to move
so much as a finger.

Shocked by her father's harsh manner, Miranda pleaded,
"Have pity, father! Surely this youth is innocent of any wrong."

"Do you think him worthy of your attention?" Prospero
asked. "There are plenty more and better."

"Yes, I judge him worthy," she insisted.

"Nonsense!" replied Prospero, and turning to the prince, he
said, "Now come along. You have no power to resist me."

"Apparently not," Ferdinand conceded, for try as he might,
he could not resist. Yet as he followed, he made every effort to
look back toward Miranda, saying, "Gladly I would be his prisoner if I could gaze upon this fair maiden once a day!"

At the same time, the rebellious Caliban was making a drawn-out labor of gathering wood. Ariel, watching from high above, saw that Caliban had not collected so much as a single stick.

"I know you're here to scold me for being late with the wood," Caliban grumbled, sensing that some spirit was near. "Horrid spirits that come and pinch me and pull my hair and never show your-selves!" Then, suddenly hearing footsteps, Caliban flung himself on the ground and hid under his rough woodbark cloak.

The footsteps belonged to the king's jester, Trinculo, whose only thought was to find shelter in case of another storm. But at the sight of the unusual cloak with hairy feet peeking out one end and hairy hands peeking out the other, the jester stopped in his tracks.

"What have we here?" wondered Trinculo. "Man, is it, or fish? From the smell I'd say fish! And dead, I'd wager, by the stink."

Circling the mysterious heap, Trinculo investigated. "Hmm . . . it's too large for any ordinary fish. I know! It's a sea monster washed up by the storm! Oh, if only I was home where people would pay good money to see a monster."

Ariel, much amused by the foolery, now caused the sky to rumble ominously.

"Goodness!" cried the jester, horrified. "Will the weather never cease to threaten me? Soon it will be pouring rain." Holding his nose to shut out Caliban's foul smell, Trinculo hastily crawled under the cloak for shelter.

In the next moment, Trinculo's friend, the king's butler, Stephano, came walking by. The sight of the sprawling creature with four legs and four arms caused him to stop and stare in wonder.

"When I am rescued," he thought aloud, making ambitious plans, "I will bring this monster back to my homeland, and for such a rare discovery I shall become as rich as a king!"

But lifting the cloak, Stephano discovered with a cry of surprise that half of the limbs belonged to his dear friend Trinculo. Joyfully, the reunited companions embraced and began to skip and dance in a mad circle.

The equally astonished Caliban decided that these gaily costumed beings must be gods fallen from the heavens after the wild tempest. He flung himself at their feet, saying, "I'll serve you, my good masters! I'll take you to the honey hives and freshwater streams and show you where the sweetest berries grow. . . only, you must rid me of Prospero."

The butler and jester did not have to be persuaded. "Henceforth you shall address me as 'Your Royal Master,'" Stephano instructed Caliban, imitating the manner of royalty. "And the good Trinculo shall be referred to in exactly the same fashion. Now lead us to this ruffian Prospero!"

"We will make short work of him!" boasted Trinculo.

But as the three set out, Ariel called upon the other sprites, instructing them to see to it that Caliban and his newfound masters should encounter no end of misery.

Meanwhile Ferdinand was hard at work hauling rocks, as Prospero had ordered. The young prince, who was little used to such strenuous labor, was soon exhausted. Miranda begged him to rest, but he refused, saying, "I must finish before I stop, dear lady."

"Then you must allow me to help," urged Miranda. But the prince would not hear of it. Instead they became engaged in a passionate debate about whether she should assist him, so that the business of rock carrying went very slowly indeed.

Concealed in the shadows, Prospero listened with pleasure, for the task was merely set to allow the young people to get to know each other better. Indeed, Ferdinand soon openly declared, "Lady Miranda, I believe that your beauty is unequaled in all the world."

For her part, Miranda could not resist admitting that, though he was the only young man she had ever met, she wished for no other companion. In truth, the sensitive young girl saw past his handsome face and courtly manner to something deeper and more endearing that captured her heart. "But I speak too freely," she confessed.

"Freely, but also wisely," said Ferdinand. "If your words of affection are true, I should like nothing more than to make you queen of Naples when I inherit the throne."

Prospero nodded to himself in triumph, for this had been precisely his plan.

Ferdinand's earnest words brought tears to the girl's eyes and she replied, "I'm sure I am a fool to weep for what gives my heart such joy."

Finally Prospero appeared. "Fear not, my children," he said, taking both their hands. "I have heard everything and I am greatly pleased. Ferdinand, let me make amends by giving my approval to the marriage between you and my daughter."

But others were not faring as well. Prospero's brother Antonio and the king of Naples, Alonso, had been wandering the island for hours. Worn out, they collapsed on the beach in despair. Suddenly, from out of thin air, a splendid feast appeared.

"Do my eyes deceive me?" cried the king, looking upon the wonderful meal.

"Say no more. It is a miracle. Now let us eat," answered Antonio.

But when they reached out, the meal vanished amid thunder and lightning.

The next moment, Ariel, in the monstrous shape of a harpy, swooped down with bloodcurdling shrieks and razor-sharp talons, snapping.

Terrified, the two men covered their heads with trembling hands and buried their faces in the sand. Ignoring their cries, the harpy reminded them of their treachery in driving Prospero from his dukedom to a certain death at sea. "And for your cruel crimes against him and his infant daughter, I have come at last to punish you," declared the monster.

The two men wept bitterly and begged for mercy until the disguised Ariel deeply pitied them. Abruptly, the harpy drew up her huge, leathery wings and, rising into the sky, disappeared. Antonio and Alonso were left to look up and wonder through their tears if they had both gone mad.

ssuming a sprite's shape, Ariel returned to Prospero, and gazing at him with solemn eyes, said, "Master, your brother and the king truly regret their foul deeds against you."

"Is that so?" inquired Prospero, unconvinced.

"Yes, master," said the sprite in a rare mood of seriousness. "And I believe they have suffered enough."

"Do you, indeed," said the magician as he paused and studied the spirit. Ariel's words forced him to weigh compassion for his enemies against his all-consuming desire for revenge. Had he not planned two harrowing days of suffering for his brother and the king? Should he instead cut it short and heed the advice of Ariel, who had no malice?

The old man sighed heavily. "You may be right, my dear Ariel. Perhaps I am reconciled at last. Bring them to me, my good spirit, so I may see for myself."

In a flash, Ariel returned in the form of a pack of howling wolves, chasing the frightened king and Antonio. Grief and terror so affected their senses that they fell to their knees before Prospero, neither man recognizing him.

"Has it been so long?" asked Prospero as he looked down upon them. At the sound of his voice, instantly both men knew him.

Taking hold of the hem of Prospero's robe, the king cried, "I know I have done you a great wrong, and though I have not earned your forgiveness, the fates have meted out just punishment. I have lost my only son in the tempest and have faced such torment that my life will never be the same. I swear that ever after I will uphold your right to the throne of Milan."

Then Antonio, with tears in his eyes, implored his brother's forgiveness. "I promise to restore your dukedom to you and if another attempts to take what is yours, I will lay down my life to protect it."

To their very great surprise, Prospero forgave them. "But there is still a greater reward for your repentance," said the enchanter, and he drew back the curtain in front of his cave to reveal Miranda and Ferdinand tenderly holding hands.

That evening Prospero summoned a magnificent pageant of fairies to celebrate the wedding of Miranda and the prince. And to the strains of soft music, the three goddesses Ceres, Iris, and Juno descended from the heavens to bestow gifts of contentment and harmony upon the joyful couple.

At the close of the wedding festivities, a bedraggled Caliban, Trinculo, and Stephano stumbled into the group. They had been led into several swamps by Ariel's fellow sprites, who had then turned themselves into an angry swarm of hornets that chased and stung the pitiful men. Now Caliban fell to his knees and begged Prospero's forgiveness, as the jester and butler tried without success to appear dignified before the king.

At last the ship's crew was summoned and the ship restored. Amid preparations to leave the enchanted island, Prospero looked with affection on the carefree Ariel who for so long had done his bidding. A sprite's is the purest of natures, he thought—wild and innocent of all human grievances. Quietly he put away his robe and staff forever. No more would his magic enslave this isle of immortals— nor another mortal soul.

Once onboard ship for Milan, Prospero never looked back. Willingly he took up the life of an ordinary man, spending his last years among his own people in the land where he was born. He watched with pleasure as Miranda and Ferdinand prospered. Gladly he helped in the rearing of his grandchildren, trusting that they would one day grow into better adults than those he had known and make a better world than the one that had been.

As for the spirit Ariel, freedom was joyous. Flying with the other sprites hither and yon across their beloved isle, which at long last was restored to them, they sang this joyous song:

Where the bee drinks, there drink I
In cowslip's bell I lie
There I crouch when owls do cry
On the bat's back I do fly
After summer merrily
Merrily, merrily, shall I live now
Under the blossom that hangs on the bough.